Ela Area Public

275 Mohawk W9-BAG-135

(847) 438-3455

www.eapl.org

31241008547195

JAN -- 2016

Luigi and the Barefoot Races

Dan Paley

illustrated by **Aaron Boyd**

In summer, when the heat of the day lingers in the brick row homes on Regent Street, children play outside for as long as their parents let them. Parents sit outside too, talking with neighbors about the good old days as they crack sunflower seeds and drink home-made iced tea. Boys and girls gather in the street for their favorite summertime sport: barefoot races.

No one knows why the kids race barefoot. Some think it's because running shoes cost too much money. Others think it's because the kids throw all their shoes up on the telephone wires. But whenever anyone asked Luigi Lenzini, the legendary barefoot racer of Regent Street just said, "Shoes slow you down."

uigi Lenzini wasn't very tall. And he wasn't very strong. But he was fast. He was so fast that he won every race he ever ran. No one could beat him. No one ever came close. Except once.

One day, a kid from another neighborhood challenged Luigi to a race. His name was Mikey Muldoon. He was fast too. He had long legs and took long strides. He also had a humongous head that leaned forward as he ran, helping him to pick up speed but making it hard for him to stop. Luigi accepted the challenge and the race was on.

Children from the neighborhood lined both sides of the street to get a good view. Off in the distance, at the finish line, stood the very tall judge, Mr. McFarland. Luigi and Mikey took off their shoes, stretched out their long, skinny toes, and walked up to the starting line. Mr. McFarland held up a bright red flag. "On your marks, get set, GO!" Mr. McFarland dropped the flag and the barefoot boys bolted off the line.

efore long, Luigi was way out in front of Mikey. He was ten paces ahead by the halfway point at the big spruce tree, and twenty paces ahead by the time he tagged Mr. McFarland's outstretched hand at the finish line.

No one was surprised. Not Luigi or Mr. McFarland, not the parents on the front steps, and not the kids watching from the sidewalks. The only one who might have been surprised was Mikey Muldoon. But he wasn't. Instead, he was mad. Steaming mad.

It took him a little while to slow down; his head had carried him halfway down the next block. But by the time he made his way back he had a new challenge for Luigi.

"You're not that fast, Luigi," shouted Mikey. "That was a lucky win."

"Want to race again?" replied Luigi.

"No, I don't want to race you again," puffed Mikey, "but I will challenge you to another race."

"What do you mean?" asked Luigi.

"I challenge you to race my best friend," said Mikey.

"Your best friend? Sure, I'll race him," said Luigi, "and I'll win just like I did today."

"You have to promise that you will race him when I bring him here tomorrow," demanded Mikey. "No matter what."

"I promise," said Luigi.

The next day Regent Street was buzzing with excitement. Again, kids from the neighborhood lined the sidewalks to watch the big race. All the parents were out in front of their houses, cracking sunflower seeds and drinking iced tea. Luigi was there, too, in his lucky striped shirt. The only ones not there were Mikey Muldoon and his best friend.

Suddenly there was a commotion as the crowd began to make way for someone. It was Mikey Muldoon and his best friend.

Some kids gasped. Others ran away. Finally, the two of them made it through the crowd and to the starting line. Luigi was shocked. His toes trembled in his shoes.

Mikey's best friend was none other than Mean Max!

Mean Max was, well, mean. Everyone in the neighborhood was afraid of him.

"I'm not racing him!" shouted Luigi.

"But you promised," said Mikey.

"But I'm afraid of him," said Luigi.

"A promise is a promise," said Mikey.

Luigi couldn't break his promise, so he agreed to race. Some kids ran back home to get their brothers and sisters. Others hollered and waved and banged on doors up and down Regent Street. Some of the boys and girls climbed on cars to get a better view.

Down the street at the finish line stood Mr. McFarland, tall as a telephone pole. At the starting line stood a scary Mean Max and a scared Luigi Lenzini. This was the closest Luigi had ever been to Max. He seemed bigger up close. Luigi could hear his heavy breathing.

Mr. McFarland raised his bright red flag and said, "On your marks, get set—"

"Wait!" shouted Salvatore, Luigi's little brother. "You forgot to take off your shoes!"

Luigi had been so afraid of Mean Max that he had forgotten to go barefoot. He quickly sat down on the curb, took off his shoes, and stretched out his long skinny toes. Now he was ready to race.

Luigi walked back to the starting line and took his place next to Mean Max. Once again Mr. McFarland raised his bright red flag: "On your marks, get set, GO!"

uigi Lenzini and Mean Max darted off the starting line, stretching their legs as they raced down the street. They passed Hubie Hess's house and were even. They passed Baxter Bonner's house and were even still. They passed Seal Slocum's house and were still even. Then they passed Paulie Pollack's house, but they were no longer side by side.

Now Mean Max was winning!

This was the first time Luigi Lenzini had ever seen the back of an opponent and he didn't like it one bit. He stretched his toes longer and longer and churned his bare feet faster and faster. He started to catch up to Mean Max. But would there be enough time?

"I can't lose!" thought Luigi.
"Not to mean old Max!"

As they passed the giant spruce tree, Luigi caught up with Mean Max and they were again neck and neck. The finish line was next. They could see Mr. McFarland with his hands up, waiting for the winner's tag. With 20 paces left Luigi was ahead. With 10 paces left Mean Max was ahead. Luigi sucked in another breath and spun his little legs faster than he ever had before. Luigi. Max. Luigi. Max. Luigi. Max. Luigi! Luigi!

Luigi wins again!

Luigi jumped in the air! The whole street erupted in cheers.
"Luigi wins again!" they shouted. "Luigi wins again!"

Even the parents smiled with puffy cheeks full of sunflower seeds.

Mean Max walked slowly over to his best friend, Mikey Muldoon. Both were sad to have lost. And as they began to leave, the judge, Mr. McFarland, declared Luigi Lenzini the winner.

Then he added one new rule for the barefoot races: "No more dogs allowed in my races!"

Luigi was happy Mean Max was back on his leash.

He was still the best barefoot racer on Regent Street.

No one could beat him. Not a boy. Not a girl. Not even a dog.

Tall Tales and Philadelphia

Dan Paley was raised in Philadelphia, just like his father before him and his father before him. He grew up on Regent Street, watching barefoot races from his front stoop. His best friend was a boy named Luigi who really was the fastest kid in the neighborhood. Dan had to learn that the hard way again and again . . . and again. But was Luigi fast enough to beat a dog? Or is *Luigi and the Barefoot Races* just a tall tale written to delight everyone who has ever felt like an underdog?

What's a Tall Tale?

A tall tale is a story that seems too amazing to be true. *A boy beat a dog in a foot race?* That definitely qualifies as a tall tale. After all, dogs are really fast. They have twice as many legs as humans! But here's the thing about tall tales: They are based on real events even if things get exaggerated a bit. Maybe Dan's story is true or maybe it's a modern-day tall tale of Philadelphia. You'll have to decide what to believe.

Tall tales are filled with incredible feats of strength, speed, and courage. But even when a story is hard to believe, it helps us to understand the place and culture it describes. For example, the story of Luigi and Mean Max is helpful if you want to understand the "underdog" mentality that many people from Philadelphia identify with.

You see, Luigi wasn't the strongest kid or the tallest kid, and we don't even know how he did in school, but he kept his word and did his best. Underdogs have heart and courage, and when they're up against "the big dogs," they go all out! Whether it's a hockey game between the Philadelphia Flyers and the New York Rangers or a debate about the historical importance of the city, Philadelphia's citizens have a lot of pride and sometimes feel their city doesn't get the respect it deserves.

When Dan was a kid, he and his friends on Regent Street had lots of opportunities to test their courage. They spent their days outside racing, jumping rope, exploring Cobbs Creek, and playing tag, baseball, basketball, and football. And just like their hometown Eagles, they always wanted to win. But most of all, they wanted to compete. They wanted a good match, and they wanted to show each other how much Philly they had inside. Because every time they won, the city won, too.

PHILADELPHIA FACTS

* Philadelphia is the second largest city on America's East Coast (after New York, of course!) and the fifth largest in the country.

* America's democracy is rooted in Philadelphia. It's where the Constitution of the United States of America was written and where the Liberty Bell was first rung.

* William Penn, who founded Pennsylvania as a British colony, was a member of the Society of Friends, also known as Quakers.

* Quakers are known for pacifism and social equality, and the name *Philadelphia* comes from the Greek and means City of Brotherly Love.

* The city boasts America's first library, its first hospital, and its first zoo.

Famous American Tall Tales

Paul Bunyan
Loggers used to tell stories about a superhuman frontiersman who traveled through the forests from Maine and Pennsylvania all the way to the Pacific Northwest. Paul Bunyan is always depicted as a giant of a man, and the tales celebrate his ability to handle anything from torrential rains to giant mosquitoes! Today, Paul Bunyan statues can be found in many places including Portland, Oregon, and Bemidji, Minnesota. The world's largest Paul Bunyan statue—31 feet tall and weighing 3,700 pounds—was built in 1959 in Bangor, Maine. Paul Bunyan statues often show him with an axe or his ox—Babe the Blue Ox.

Pecos Bill
If you travel into cowboy country, you might hear the legend of Pecos Bill. The story goes that this hero was raised by coyotes who rescued him from drowning in the Pecos River. He became famous for cattle branding and calf roping, and statues of Pecos Bill often show him with a lariat in his hand. One such statue is in Washington, D.C., just outside the Museum of American Art/National Portrait Gallery.

John Henry
Many songs featuring the story of John Henry, "the Steel-Driving Man," have been recorded by blues, folk, and even rock musicians. But there was a *real* African-American man named John Henry who lived in the 1870s and worked on the building of railway tunnels. According to legend, his heart gave out after he won a race against a steam-powered hammer. A statue stands in his honor in the town of Talcott, West Virginia, which holds a John Henry Days festival each year.

Molly Pitcher
There is debate about who the "real" Molly Pitcher was. Some have said that General George Washington thanked her for her bravery in firing a cannon during the battle of Monmouth in the Revolutionary War. Others say that Molly Pitcher was a nickname for *all* the women who helped fight the British by giving water to thirsty soldiers. Official rest stops on the New Jersey Turnpike are named for famous people who lived (or died) there, and southbound travelers may get coffee at a rest stop named for Molly Pitcher.

Rocky Balboa
This is the ultimate underdog story, and of course it's set in Philadelphia! *Rocky* is a film series that features the life and times of a small-time boxer from working-class Philly. Sylvester Stallone debuted the Rocky Balboa story in 1976, and it has continued ever since. A statue of Rocky stands at the front steps of the Philadelphia Museum of Art and is one of the most popular tourist attractions in the city.

TRY THIS!

Invent a Tall Tale
Break into groups and brainstorm the best adventures you have shared with friends or family. Then pick an "unlikely" kid to be the hero of that adventure and have him or her participate in an unbelievable event. Make the story as vivid as possible and give it a happy ending. Write the story and illustrate it.

Celebrate the "Underdog"—Site and Design a Statue
Cities and towns are full of monuments that tell stories to honor their heroes. Explore your community and learn about its monuments. Imagine a place in your community where a statue to honor a local underdog might be welcome! Next, design a monument to your chosen underdog for display in your community. If statues of Paul Bunyan have an axe, and Molly Pitcher had a pitcher, what would your statue need?

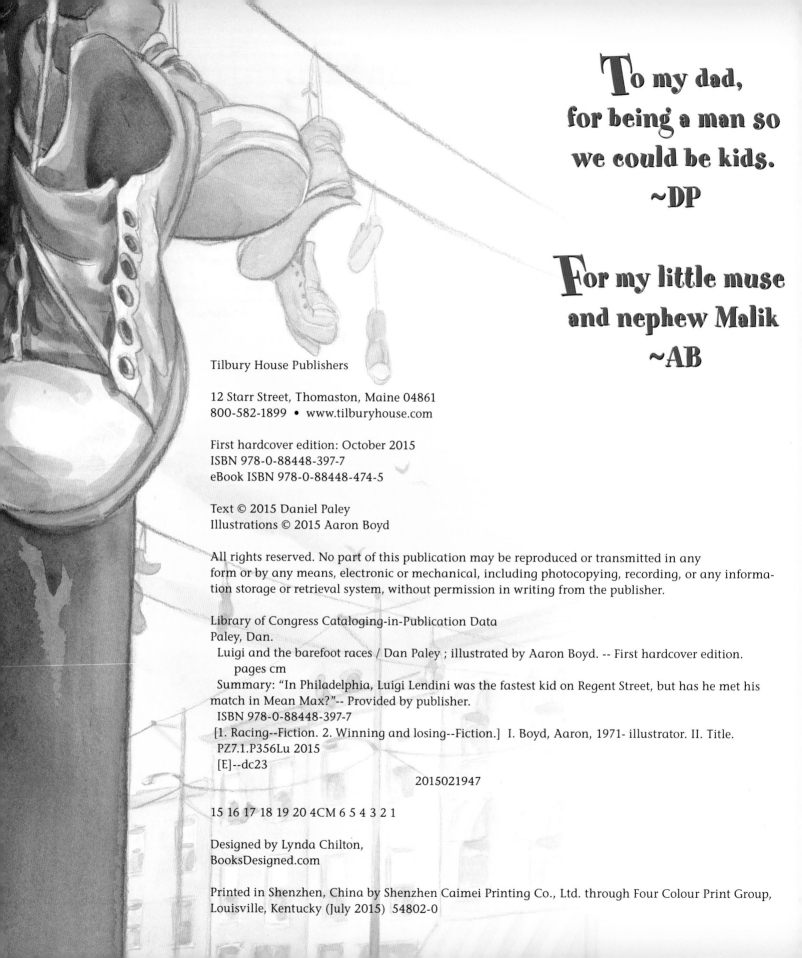

To my dad,
for being a man so
we could be kids.
~DP

For my little muse
and nephew Malik
~AB

Tilbury House Publishers

12 Starr Street, Thomaston, Maine 04861
800-582-1899 • www.tilburyhouse.com

First hardcover edition: October 2015
ISBN 978-0-88448-397-7
eBook ISBN 978-0-88448-474-5

Text © 2015 Daniel Paley
Illustrations © 2015 Aaron Boyd

All rights reserved. No part of this publication may be reproduced or transmitted in any form or by any means, electronic or mechanical, including photocopying, recording, or any information storage or retrieval system, without permission in writing from the publisher.

Library of Congress Cataloging-in-Publication Data
Paley, Dan.
  Luigi and the barefoot races / Dan Paley ; illustrated by Aaron Boyd. -- First hardcover edition.
    pages cm
  Summary: "In Philadelphia, Luigi Lendini was the fastest kid on Regent Street, but has he met his match in Mean Max?"-- Provided by publisher.
  ISBN 978-0-88448-397-7
  [1. Racing--Fiction. 2. Winning and losing--Fiction.] I. Boyd, Aaron, 1971- illustrator. II. Title.
  PZ7.1.P356Lu 2015
  [E]--dc23

                        2015021947

15 16 17 18 19 20 4CM 6 5 4 3 2 1

Designed by Lynda Chilton,
BooksDesigned.com

Printed in Shenzhen, China by Shenzhen Caimei Printing Co., Ltd. through Four Colour Print Group, Louisville, Kentucky (July 2015) 54802-0